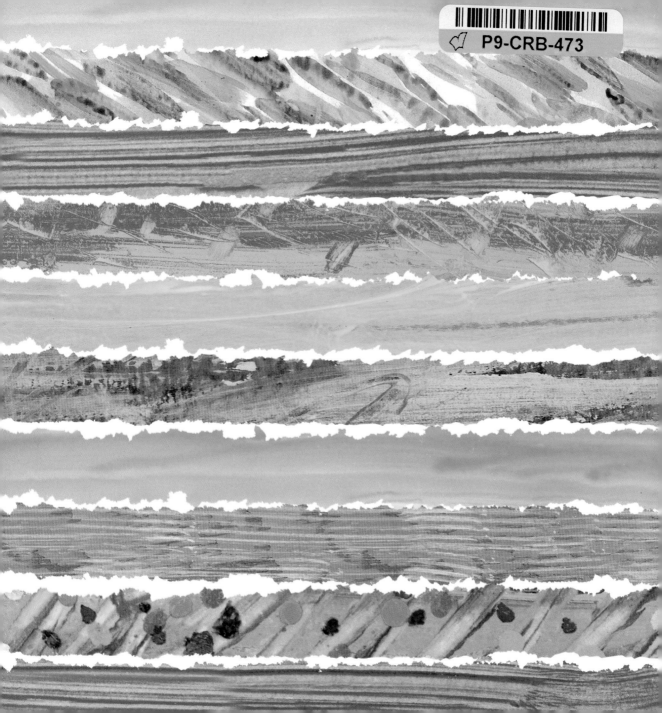

Kindergarten 2021 Jocelyn Beaudoin

Joce, noodles, spot

So my little BFF, I don't know what to say. I'm going to miss you, our friday Karen/Joce days. From going to the beach in winter, to going to the crazy lady for getting our nails done, going to the park or store. Breakfast (the way you love your eggs). Our (the Eames) will not ever be the same since you were born. You better come for visits. I will miss your love of make-up & and your gorgeous hair. The way you help everyone of our babies and always finding a way to make us smile. You are so smart. Keep cooking, keep loving everything that you do. with such enjoyment & grace as you do. your dancing & making up your own songs to everything. Love, Karen

I could keep writing for ever about you!

You Are Ready!
The World Is Waiting

Always Remember

You Are Amazing!

You Are IMPORTANT!

You Are SPECIAL!

You Are UNIQUE!

You Are KIND!

YOU ARE PRECIOUS!

YOU ARE BEAUTIFUL!

You ARE Loved!

By Eric Carle

HARPER

An Imprint of HarperCollinsPublishers

You

are

ready.

It's time for you to

spread

your

wings.

The **world**

can seem like a scary place.

But
you
are
ready.

You have
everything
you need
inside you.

You
are
stronger
than you know.

Be a
light
in the
darkness.

Reach

high

when you feel

low.

Make
friends

wherever you go.

When you feel lost,

be **true**

to **yourself...**

. . . and you'll always

find

your way

home.

So **ready, set...**

into the world

you go!